I Love Who I Am
Self-Love For Kids

written by J. O'Keefe

Illustrated by Minnie Drew

Grace Hall Publishing, Heath, Ohio

Visit us on the Web!
www.gracehallpublishing.com

First Printing
August 2018

Published by Grace Hall Publishing.
Text copyright © 2018 by J. O'Keefe
Illustration copyright © 2018 by Grace Hall Publishing
All rights reserved. Printed in the U.S.A. First Printing May 2018
First Edition
14 13 12 11 10 / 10 9 8 7 6 5 4 3 2 1
Library of Congress Control Number: 2017949007
Paperback ISBN 978-0-9834961-0-6

Self Discovery Series For Kids

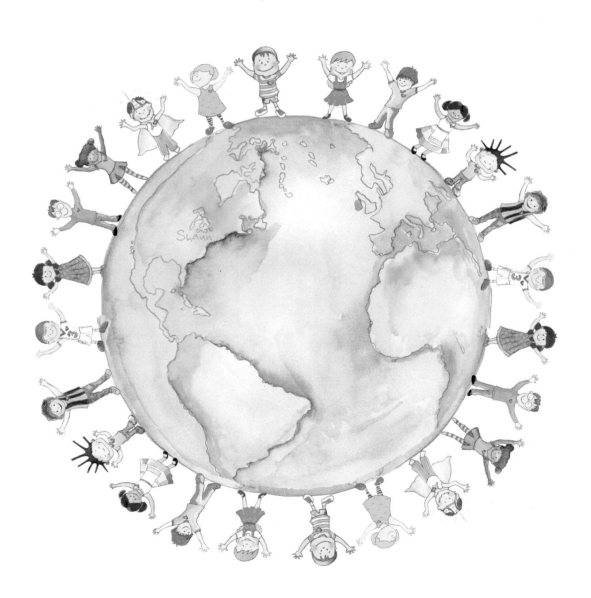

There are many people
near and far,
that do not know
just who they are.

I might be like them,
in the same jam,
the only difference is,
I LOVE who I am!

I love me when I'm happy!

I love me when I'm sad!

I love me when I'm silly!

I love me when I'm mad!

I love me when I'm good,
at baseball games and things!

I love me when I'm bad, and grow my big bats wings!

I love me in a mood,
when I don't know
what to do!

I love me in a fad,
when I try
something new!

It

really

if

this

doesn't

matter

I am

or  that.

The only thing that
matters is,
I LOVE where
I am at!

When I love who

I am I say:

yes yes

even

a

when I'm in . . .

BIG, FAT, MESS!

For love means having a
BIG OPEN HEART,
that is kind and understanding
to my each and every part.

You can do it too! Just take a little try.

With everything that happens, say:

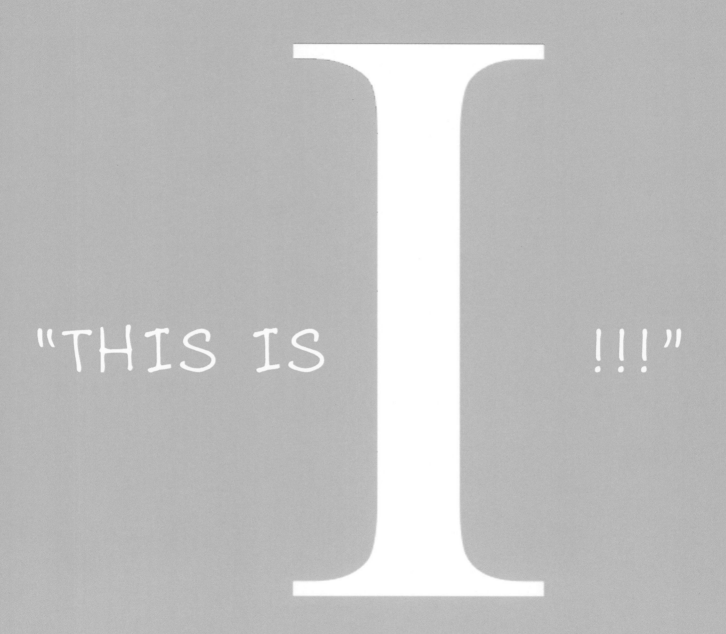

"THIS IS I !!!"

Happy, sad, silly or mad,

good, bad, in a mood, in a fad,

E S !

every feeling has a MESSAGE,

there's a GIFT in every part,

care for them ALL with

your Body, Mind and Heart,

and *loving* yourself
is off to a
great start!

Why is this important

Here's a little clue:

Learning to love ME means...

learning to love YOU!

If we ALL do this
then we are bound,

to live in a world where LOVE goes around.

Around and around

I LOVE who I am
and I LOVE
what I have found!

THE END.

..... AND THE BEGINNING

Made in the USA
Lexington, KY
31 January 2018